The Plant That Ate Dirty Socks

The Musical

Based on the book by
Nancy McArthur

Original music and
book adaptation by
Joe Iconis

A SAMUEL FRENCH ACTING EDITION

SAMUEL
FRENCH

FOUNDED 1830

SAMUELFRENCH.COM
SAMUELFRENCH-LONDON.CO.UK

FOR PRODUCTION ENQUIRIES

UNITED STATES AND CANADA

Info@SamuelFrench.com

1-866-598-8449

UNITED KINGDOM AND EUROPE

Plays@SamuelFrench-London.co.uk

020-7255-4302

Each title is subject to availability from Samuel French, depending upon country of performance. Please be aware that *THE PLANT THAT ATE DIRTY SOCKS* may not be licensed by Samuel French in your territory. Professional and amateur producers should contact the nearest Samuel French office or licensing partner to verify availability.

MUSIC USE NOTE

Licensees are solely responsible for obtaining formal written permission from copyright owners to use copyrighted music in the performance of this play and are strongly cautioned to do so. If no such permission is obtained by the licensee, then the licensee must use only original music that the licensee owns and controls. Licensees are solely responsible and liable for all music clearances and shall indemnify the copyright owners of the play(s) and their licensing agent, Samuel French, against any costs, expenses, losses and liabilities arising from the use of music by licensees. Please contact the appropriate music licensing authority in your territory for the rights to any incidental music.

RENTAL MATERIALS

An orchestration consisting of **Piano/Conductor Scores** will be loaned two months prior to the production ONLY on the receipt of the Licensing Fee quoted for all performances, the rental fee and a refundable deposit. Please contact Samuel French for perusal of the music materials as well as a performance license application.

IMPORTANT BILLING AND CREDIT REQUIREMENTS

If you have obtained performance rights to this title, please refer to your licensing agreement for important billing and credit requirements.

THE PLANT THAT ATE DIRTY SOCKS was first produced by Theatreworks USA on July 24, 2008. The performance was directed by John Simpkins, with choreography by Jennifer Werner. Sets by Michael Schweikardt, costumes by Tracy Christensen, lighting design by Chris Dallos, sound design by Eric Shim, puppet design by Eric Wright and music direction by Jana Zielonka. The production stage manager was Jeff Davolt. The cast was as follows:

MICHAEL . . . . .Jason "SweetTooth" Williams

NORMAN. . . . . Lance Rubin

MOM . . . . Lorinda Lisitza

PATTY JENKINS . . . . Lauren Marcus

JASON/MACKENZIE. . . . . .Jeffrey Omura

DAD . . . . .Kilty Reidy

CHARACTERS

NORMAN

MICHAEL

MOM

DAD

PATTY JENKINS

JASON/MACKENZIE

Scene One
Levitt Lane

(It is late afternoon on Levitt Lane. We see a mid-sized blue Suburban home. **MICHAEL** *runs on, wearing a baseball cap and dirty sneakers. He's got a small toy spaceman in his hands.)*

MICHAEL.
WOOHOO! YEAH, YEAH, YEAH, YEAH, YEAH
WOOHOO! YEAH, YEAH, YEAH, YEAH, YEAH
WOOHOO! YEAH, YEAH, YEAH, YEAH, YEAH
YEAH, YEAH, YEAH

(to the spaceman)

TODAY WAS THE FIRST DAY OF SCHOOL
THINGS WENT GOOD, THINGS WENT COOL
SEVENTH GRADE IS GONNA BE THE BEST YEAR OF ALL TIME

THE YEAR I WIN THE SPELLING BEE OR THE SCHOOL
    ELECTION
AND EVERY SMOOCHY GIRL'S AFFECTION
MAKE A TEAM OR START A ROCK BAND
BE THE MOST IMPRESSIVE GUY IN ALL THE LAND

LADIES GONNA SWOON
AND DUDES GONNA CHEER
EVERY TIME THAT I APPEAR
YEAH, IT'S GONNA HAPPEN, GONNA HAPPEN, GONNA
    HAPPEN THIS YEAR

YEAH, YEAH, YEAH, YEAH, YEAH
WOOHOO! YEAH, YEAH, YEAH, YEAH, YEAH
WOOHOO! YEAH, YEAH, YEAH, YEAH, YEAH
YEAH, YEAH, YEAH

MICHAEL. *(cont.)* Mr. Spaceman, welcome to the coolest spot in all of Levitt Lane. Kindly meet My House. And my house, kindly meet Most Sickest Spaceman Ever! Pretty sweet, huh? Dude, we're gonna have so much fun together. We're gonna do experiments and throw eggs out of windows and play Frisbee.

(**JASON** *enters, cool as cool can be. He is holding a football.*)

JASON. Michael, what are you doing? How am I supposed to decide if I'm gonna let you be my friend if you walk faster than me.

MICHAEL. Sorry, Jason, just wanted to introduce the man of space to his new home.

JASON. Are you playing with little kid toys? You're in seventh grade now. You play with footballs.

MICHAEL. But he's the most sickest Spaceman ever.

JASON. You've got so much to learn.

(**PATTY JENKINS** *enters doing a cheer. She has pom poms.*)

PATTY JENKINS. *(cheering)*
ONE-TWO-THREE-WEE!
AIN'T NOBODY GREAT AS ME
HERE'S-MY-RE-FRAIN
I'M THE BADDEST BABE ON LEVITT LANE

MICHAEL. Hey Patty.

PATTY. Did someone say my name?

MICHAEL. I did! Just wanted to say, Hi!

PATTY JENKINS. Okay – I'm gonna need you to only speak to me after I speak to you first.

JASON. *(Mr. Suave)* Hey Patty Jenkins. You know, your uniform happens to be my favorite shade of pink.

PATTY JENKINS. Really, I care. And, what are you even doing here anyway? You're not friends with Michael, what's going on here? What are you hiding?!

JASON. I felt like it would be good for my image to have a friend who was less popular than me. It'll make me seem more sensitive for the ladies. I'm just trying him out. What are you doing here?

PATTY JENKINS. I was just coming to see if Michael had picked a topic for the Levitt Lane All County Science Fair yet. Never too early to get a jump start on the competition.

(**NORMAN** *enters.*)

NORMAN. Michael!

JASON. Who is that and why is he so small?

MICHAEL. That's my little brother, Norman. Just ignore him.

NORMAN. Hello, new friends! Please to meet your acquaintance.

PATTY JENKINS. He is so pathetic.

NORMAN. Thanks!

PATTY JENKINS. Pathetic means loser.

NORMAN. Michael, where were you? I waited for twenty minutes so we could walk home from school together.

MICHAEL. Dude, we go to different schools now. I'm in Seventh Grade and you're in the Fourth Grade.

JASON. Bra, you wanna go toss the old pigskin around?

NORMAN. Nah – he's gonna help me with my vocab homework.

PATTY. Why would He help You?!

NORMAN. Cuz he already learned all the words in Mrs. Thurser's class, and besides, he's my brother!

(**NORMAN** *goes to hug* **MICHAEL,** *who recoils in shock and horror.*)

MICHAEL. Whoa, dude!

NORMAN. *(not understanding what's wrong)* What?!

(**DAD** *enters with a brief case.*)

DAD. Children! How was your first day of school, kids?

MICHAEL. Appropriately radical!

NORMAN. I was only the victim of two wedgies!

(**NORMAN** *goes inside.*)

JASON. I skipped out after second period.

DAD. *(not really listening)* Great!

MICHAEL. Jason's in Eighth Grade, Dad. He's gonna be my new friend.

JASON. Maybe.

MICHAEL. Right, maybe.

DAD. And Patty Jenkins – look at you in your cheerleading costume!

PATTY JENKINS. This isn't a costume, silly, this is a uniform! Gee, Michael's Dad, I'd expect someone as old as you to know the difference between the two!

(**MOM** *comes barreling in. She is on a cell phone and madly typing on a palm pilot at the same time.*)

MOM. *(speaking into the cell phone)* No, I have to go to Stop and Save and then I have PTA and then I have relaxation class and I don't have time for that because I don't have time for that. *(to* **DAD***)* Hi-Honey-How-Are-You?-That's-Great-Dinner-In-Five-Minutes-K?-Fantastic. *(back to the phone)* What? No, not you. Make your own dinner.

(**MOM** *starts to go into the house.*)

DAD. She is busy. She's my busy wife – who I love. Now, you kids run along, it's time for family dinner table time.

JASON. Bye, dude. Catch you later, if I feel like it.

MICHAEL. Sure thing, man! Bye, Patty.

PATTY JENKINS. Uh… Yeah, whatever.

(**PATTY** *and* **JASON** *leave.*)

MICHAEL. Did you hear that? Everybody likes me!
LADIES GONNA SWOON
AND DUDES GONNA CHEER
EVERY TIME THAT I APPEAR
YEAH, IT'S GONNA HAPPEN, GONNA HAPPEN, GONNA
  HAPPEN

EVERYONE.

IT'S GONNA HAPPEN, GONNA HAPPEN, GONNA HAPPEN

MICHAEL.

IT'S PERFECTLY CLEAR THAT IT'S GONNA HAPPEN THIS
YEAR

EVERYONE.

WOOHOO! YEAH, YEAH, YEAH, YEAH, YEAH
WOOHOO! YEAH, YEAH, YEAH, YEAH, YEAH
WOOHOO! YEAH, YEAH, YEAH, YEAH, YEAH
YEAH, YEAH, YEAH

WOOHOO! YEAH, YEAH, YEAH, YEAH, YEAH
WOOHOO! YEAH, YEAH, YEAH, YEAH, YEAH
WOOHOO! YEAH, YEAH, YEAH, YEAH, YEAH
YEAH, YEAH, YEAH, YEAH…

(**MICHAEL** *is enveloped in the dizzy explosion of First-Day-Of-School-"Anything Can Happen"-Promise. Super stoked, he runs into his room.*)

Scene Two
Michael and Norman's Room

*(We are inside the house. **MICHAEL** opens the door. One half in the room, **MICHAEL**'s side, is covered in garbage, toys, clothes, and possibly wildlife. It is literally made out of junk. The other half of the room, **NORMAN**'s side, is overly neat and minimal. **MICHAEL** sets his Spaceman down on the floor in front of his bedroom.)*

MICHAEL. *(to Spaceman)*

WELCOME TO MY ROOM, IT'S A GOOD GOOD ROOM

YOU'RE GONNA LOVE IT HERE

COMIC BOOK AND BALLS, GARBAGE CREPPING UP THE WALLS

HAVEN'T TIDIED UP SINCE THE FIRST OF THE YEAR

I DON'T MAKE MY BED

I MAKE A BIGGER MESS, INSTEAD

AND NOBODY ELSE AT LEVITT LANE JUNIOR HIGH

HAS A PAD THAT'S AS RAD, OR AS CRAZY, LAZY, WICKED, OR FLY

AS MY MY MY MY MY MY MY MY MY MY ROOM

IT'S UNLIKE ANY OTHER

NORMAN. *(offstage)* OKAY MOM!!

MICHAEL.

OH, MAN, HERE COMES MY BROTHER

*(**NORMAN** enters.)*

NORMAN. Michael – what is that?

MICHAEL. I traded Garrett Gleason my retainer for it, isn't it cool?

NORMAN. Just more garbage to add to your filth-pile!

MICHAEL. It's not garbage, this is good junk, dude.

NORMAN. I told you – one more piece of junk and that was it.

MICHAEL. What are you gonna do about it?

*(**NORMAN** gets out a roll of tape. He stretches the tapes across the floor, creating a line that separates the clean*

side of the room and the messy side. **MICHAEL** *ad libs taunting of* **NORMAN***'s taping.)*

NORMAN. There. Cross the line and I'll press charges.

MICHAEL. Uh, no you won't – you won't press charges, OK. You just won't.

NORMAN. *(interrupting)*
WELCOME TO MY ROOM, IT'S A CLEAN, CLEAN ROOM
IT IS AWFULLY NEAT
EVERY PENCIL'S IN IT'S PLACE, NOT A TOUCH OF
    CLUTTERED SPACE
AND IT DOESN'T SMELL LIKE STINKY FEET
WITH TAPE I MADE A LINE
TO SEPARATE YOUR ROOM FROM MINE

MICHAEL.
OO, I'M GONNA CROSS IT!

NORMAN.
OH, I'D LIKE TO SEE YOU TRY

MICHAEL.
YOU GEEK

NORMAN.
YOU REEK!
SEE, THERE'S SCHOOLS OF RULES I PROUDLY APPLY
TO MY MY MY MY MY MY MY MY MY MY ROOM

*(***MICHAEL** *flings the spaceman on a pile of junk.* **DAD** *enters.)*

DAD. Hello, my little young men.

MICHAEL/NORMAN. Hi, Dad/Daddy!

*(***MOM** *enters. She is carrying a laundry basket and is wearing an oven mitt.)*

MOM. *(to* **DAD***)* What are you, doing? The roast is cold. *(to* **MICHAEL***)* The mess is getting bigger.

MICHAEL. *(proud)* Thanks for noticing, Mom!

NORMAN. He just got another piece of trash, too.

MICHAEL. Junk, Norman, it's called junk, not trash!

MOM. Your father and I are not happy with the state of this room. Your father is furious, in fact. Look at him.

DAD. You know Michael, it's good that you collect all these things –

MOM. Good? How is it good?

DAD. And it's good that you have all these hobbies –

MOM. Too many hobbies, too many things –

DAD. But your mother and I are very concerned.

MOM. You never apply yourself, you just don't apply!

DAD. We just think you're not working up to your potential.

MICHAEL. But I have lots of potential – look I have a whole pile of it.

MOM. Are those your dirty socks hanging on that lamp?

MICHAEL. I was baking the stink out of them!

MOM. If there is one thing I can't stand it's when you leave your dirty socks all over the place.

NORMAN. I can't live like this anymore. Can't we get rid of Michael and get a dog instead?

DAD. My boy has been wanting a dog for a quite a while! I think a schnauzer might do us some good! Honey?

MOM. We don't have time for a dog, right now. Dog later. Dinner now.

DAD. I guess I see your point.

(**MOM** *and* **DAD** *leave.*)

PAPERBOY. *(offstage)* Mail Delivery for Mr. Michael!

(*A huge stack of mail comes flying through the bedroom window.*)

MICHAEL. Woo-hoo!

(**MICHAEL** *leafs through his mail.*)

NORMAN. *(calling out the window)* Anything for me?

PAPERBOY. *(offstage)* Nope – same as every other day! No mail for you! Have a good one!

NORMAN. I think our mail delivery boy is really rude.

MICHAEL. Dude, I got a ton of super cool cereal-box sendaways. Look – styrofoam airplane, sweet. Weirdo purpley racing car, sweet. And –

(**MICHAEL** *holds up a mysterious looking box.* **NORMAN** *is intrigued.*)

NORMAN. A magically mysterious looking box!

MICHAEL. I don't remember sending away for this.

(**MICHAEL** *opens up the box and takes out a sheet of paper.*)

MOM/DAD/PAPERBOY/MICHAEL.
HERE ARE THE AMAZING BEANS YOU ORDERED
HERE ARE THE AMAZING BEANS YOU ORDERED

NORMAN. Where did those come from?

MICHAEL. I don't know! I don't remember ordering them.

NORMAN. Well, keep reading!

MICHAEL/MOM/DAD/PAPERBOY.
TREAT THIS SHEET WITH CAUTION AND CARE
FOLLOW THE DIRECTIONS AND BEWARE

MICHAEL/MOM/DAD/PAPERBOY/NORMAN.
IF YOU IGNORE THE NEEDS OF THE SEEDS IN THIS BOX
THE PLANTS THEY YEILD WILL BE REVEALED TO BE
THE PLANTS WITH THE POWER TO DEVOUR ALL YOUR –

(**MICHAEL** *crumples up the paper and throws it into the trash heap.*)

NORMAN. Why'd you do that for?!

MICHAEL. I dunno. Boring. Let's plant these babies. Chill, Norm. Here.

(**MICHAEL** *puts a bean into* **NORMAN***'s hands.*)

You can plant one and I'll plant one.

NORMAN. Really? You really think a Fourth Grader is grown-up enough to care for a living thing?

MICHAEL. It's just a plant, dude.

NORMAN. You're going to be the neatest plant in the whole world.

MICHAEL.
I'M GONNA PUT MINE BY THE WINDOW
GIVE IT SUN AND QUENCH IT'S THIRST

NORMAN.

> I'LL PUT MINE BY THE WINDOW ALSO
> BUT NOT BECAUSE YOU SAID IT FIRST
>
> I'M GONNA USE MY SUPER BLASTER
> TO WATER UNTIL THE FIRST BUD COMES

MICHAEL.

> I'M GONNA MAKE MINE GROW MUCH FASTER
> FEED IT PIZZA AND CUPCAKE CRUMBS

NORMAN.

> WELL IF YOURS OOZES OVER THE LINE
> MINE WILL BEAT IT UP

MICHAEL.

> OH, I'M SHAKING IN MY PANTS
> YOURS WILL NEVER BE AS STRONG AS MINE
>
> (**MOM** *pops in with the laundry basket. She pops around the room picking up stray socks.*)

MOM. Just what we need – dueling plants!

> (**MICHAEL** *and* **NORMAN** *plant their seeds, using dirt from a sack of soil found in the bottom of* **MICHAEL**'s *junk pile, and two huge oversize pencil holders from* **NORMAN**'s *desk.*)

MICHAEL & NORMAN.

> WELCOME TO MY ROOM, IT'S AN AWESOME ROOM
> ONE THAT'S AWESOMER THAN MOST
> AND I'VE NEVER HAD A PLANT BUT
> THAT DOESN'T MEAN I CAN'T BE A KILLER HOST
> THIS ROOM'S A ROOM THAT ROCKS

MICHAEL.

> EXCEPT FOR SOMETIMES WHEN I CAN'T FIND MY SOCKS

MOM. You know, they're missing cuz you just throw them around the room! One day, Michael, your leaving socks around the room just might get you into a boat load of trouble, Mister. Maybe, one day very, very, soon. ...2,3,4 –

> (**MOM** *leaves.*)

NORMAN. *(to* **THE PLANT***)*
> I'M GLAD YOU EXIST

MICHAEL.
> I'M GONNA BE THE GREATEST HORTICULTURIST

NORMAN.
> IN MY MY MY MY MY MY MY MY

MICHAEL.
> MY MY MY MY MY MY MY MY

NORMAN.
> MY MY MY MY MY MY MY MY

MICHAEL.
> MY MY MY MY MY MY MY MY

MICHAEL & NORMAN.
> MY MY MY MY MY MY MY MY
> MY MY MY MY MY MY MY MY
> MY MY MY MY MY MY MY MY
> ROOM!
> YEAH!

Scene Three
One Week Later

*(The **PLANTS** have grown to the size of full grown, normal, everyday, nothin-special house plants. Something about them is weird, though. Off-kilter. Strange. **NORMAN** and **MICHAEL** are eating pizza and playing video games. **JASON** is oogling the plants.)*

MICHAEL. Hey, dude! Pretty cool, right? Totally the kind of things guys like us have in their bedroom.

JASON. These plants are way weird. They look like they have antennae.

NORMAN. Shhh! You'll hurt their feelings. *(calling out)* Jason didn't mean it, Fluffy!

JASON. You named your plant Fluffy?!

MICHAEL. Norman, stop being all geeky in front of the guest.

NORMAN. I am not being geeky. I'm being nerd-ish. Big, huge difference.

(A bell rings.)

MICHAEL & NORMAN. Feeding time!

*(**NORMAN** gets out his super soaker water pistol and carefully administers three shots of water into **FLUFFY**'s soil. **MICHAEL** tosses his pizza crust into his plant's pot.)*

JASON. Whoa! You feed your plant pizza?

MICHAEL. That's why he's stronger and bigger than that one over there!

NORMAN. Fatter and dumber is more like it – you're not supposed to feed a plant pizza, Michael.

MICHAEL. I don't just feed it pizza – I feed it potato chips, too! And what are you doing?

NORMAN. This year for the Levitt Lane All County Science Fair, I'm charting my plant's growth by watering it three ounces every day. *(to **MICHAEL**)* This is good, right?

JASON. *(making fun of him)* You've already thought about the science fair?

NORMAN. Yeah, so has Michael!

MICHAEL. No I haven't!

NORMAN. Sure you have!

JASON. Well, well, well, I didn't realize you were so serious about the science fair, Mr. Science Man.

MICHAEL. Well, I am, sorta. The science fair is totally cool. And this year, I'm going all the way.

> I'M GON' ROCK THE SCIENCE FAIR WITH A PROJECT THAT'S SO BIG
> AN ELECTRICAL WHIP OR ROCKET SHIP OR A FOIL OIL RIG
> OR A PERFECT COMBINATION OF EVERY SINGLE THING I DIG
> AND THEN I'LL SAY
> HEY SUCKA-SUCKA-YEAH, HAVEN'T YOU HEARD
> THAT I WON THE SCIENCE FAIR
> YEAH, THAT I WON THE SCIENCE FAIR
> OH-OH-OH
> OH-OH-OH

NORMAN.

> IF I WON THE SCIENCE FAIR I'D BE NUMBER ONE KING NERD

MICHAEL.

> ALL THE DWEEBS AND GEEKS WOULD WORSHIP THEE
> AND REVERE YOUR EVERY WORD

NORMAN.

> AND IF ANY STUPID BULLY TRIED TO ROUGH ME UP I'D SAY, HEY –
> BACK OFF BIG MAN, HAVEN'T YOU HEARD
> THAT I WON THE SCIENCE FAIR

NORMAN & MICHAEL.

> YEAH, THAT I WON THE SCIENCE FAIR
> OH-OH-OH, OH-OH-OH

JASON. OK, I'm gonna go.

MICHAEL. Wait, wait, wait, wait, what's wrong?!

JASON. Listen, man, this just isn't working out. The two of you getting all excited about the Dork Fair, it's just not the sort of image that I need to be associating myself with.

MICHAEL. Wait, no, I was only kidding about that stuff.

JASON. Really?

MICHAEL. Of course. I mean –
> IF I WON THE SCIENCE FAIR, I KNOW WHAT I WOULD DO
> I'D USE MY NEW-FOUND CLOUT TO SHOUT ABOUT HOW I'M
>   SO MUCH BETTER THAN ALL OF YOU
> I'D BOP AND HOP FROM CHICK TO CHICK LIKE A SUPA-
>   COOL KANGAROO
> WOO!
> WHEN I WIN THE SCI –

NORMAN. What are you talking about, Michael?

JASON. He's talking like a sensible man. Don't you want to be popular?

NORMAN. I want people to like me for who I am, thank you very much.

JASON. Well, all I know is, Science is Dumb.

MICHAEL. You're just jealous cuz we're not freakazoid nerds and you are.

JASON. Good one. You're really getting the hang of this.

NORMAN. Well, fine. You just wait –
> WHEN I WIN THE SCIENCE FAIR,
> I'LL WIELD MY TROPHY LIKE A SWORD
> EVERY KID IN SCHOOL WILL THINK I'M COOL
> I'LL NO LONGER BE IGNORED
> AND EVEN THOUGH I'M STILL A DWEEB,
> NO DWEEB WILL BE MORE ADORED

MICHAEL.
> WHEN I WIN THE SCIENCE FAIR

MICHAEL/NORMAN.	**JASON.**
(overlapping)	*(overlapping)*
WHEN I WIN THE SCIENCE FAIR	I DON'T CARE ABOUT THE SCIENCE FAIR
WHEN I WIN THE SCIENCE FAIR	I DON'T CARE ABOUT THE SCIENCE FAIR

MICHAEL/NORMAN.
　　WHEN I WIN THE SCIENCE FAIR!
JASON.
　　OH-OH-OH
MICHAEL/NORMAN.
　　OH-OH-OH-OH-OH
　　YEAH!

JASON. *(to* **MICHAEL***)* Okay. By my calculation, we have now entered the final round of this friendship trial. Either we do something fun, or I leave.

MICHAEL. Yeah. Sure. Whatever you want.

JASON. Good! So now we're gonna go outside and chase squirrels.

MICHAEL. Perfect! That was just gonna be the thing I was planning on making a suggestion about.

　　(JASON, MICHAEL, *and* **NORMAN** *jump up and start to leave.)*

JASON. Where do you think you're going?

NORMAN. I thought we were gonna run with the squirrels! Are we not gonna run with the squirrels, cuz that's fine too.

JASON. Aw – he thinks he was invited. That is so sad.

MICHAEL. Yeah.

　　(They start to leave.)

NORMAN. *(like "C'mon.")* Mike.

　　(MICHAEL *makes a face like "Sorry…but I can't help it." He shrugs and leaves.* **NORMAN** *is left alone. He looks around his room.)*

Oh, Fluffy. No one ever wants to do stuff with me. Even my brother. We used to be friends and stuff. Now he won't even stick up for me. But you – you're not like that at all. Look at you – you're loyal, and fun to be around, and nice.
SOME PEOPLE CAN'T HAVE A BIRD
CUZ BIRDS MAKE 'EM SNIFFLE AND SNEEZE
OTHERS THINK FISH ARE BEST SERVED ON A DISH
AND OTHERS HATE DOGS ON ACCOUNT OF THE FLEAS

NORMAN. *(cont.)*
> BUT TO THESE PET-LESS FOLKS I SAY
> IF ON YOUR WAY HOME FROM WORK TODAY
> YOU HAPPEN TO PASS YOUR LOCAL GARDEN SHOP
> THEN STOP
>
> BECAUSE, PLANTS MAKE PERFECTLY PRICKLY
> PLEASANTLY TICKLY PETS
>
> EVERYBODY FORGETS
> PLANTS MAKE WONDERFUL PETS
>
> A PLANT WOULD NEVER SNAP OR HISS
> LIKE A SNAKE OR A FOUL-MOUTHED PUG
> THEY DON'T GET THEIR HAIRS ON ORANGE CHAIRS
> OR MAKE A LITTER BOX OUT OF THE RUG
>
> NO, NO PLANTS MAKE EXTRA EXOTICAL,
> SOMETIMES AQCAUTICAL PETS
> RARELY UNRAVEL CASSETTES
> PLANTS MAKE WONDERFUL PETS
>
> SOME PEOPLE GET TEASED AT SCHOOL
> CUZ THEY AREN'T GOOD AT SPORTS
> THEY DO WELL ON TESTS, BUT DESPITE THEIR REQUESTS
> THEY EAT LUNCH ON THEIR OWN, AND ARE LONERS OF
>   SORTS
>
> BUT TO THESE NERDY KIDS, I GIVE YOU HOPE
> FLOWERS GROW ON THE GYM CLASS ROPE
> AND IF AT BATTING PRACTICE
> YOUR PERFORMANCE WAS LAME
> GO BUY A CACTUS
> AND GIVE IT A NAME
> AND THINGS WILL NEVER BE THE SAME

NORMAN.	**ALL OTHERS.**
YOU SEE,	
PLANTS MAKE	BOP-BOP-BOP-BOP
BACK-YOU-UP-FULLY AND	OOO-OOO
NEVER-WILL-BULLY-YOU	OOO-OOO-BOP-BOP-BOP
FRIENDS	
You're dancin', Fluff!	
IT'S THE	OOO-OOO
LATEST OF TRENDS	LATEST OF TRENDS

ALL.

> PLANTS MAKE WONDERFUL
> PLANTS MAKE PERFECTLY PRICKLY
> PLEASANTLY TICKLY PETS
> EVERYBODY FORGETS
> PLANTS MAKE WONDERFUL
> PLANTS MAKE WONDERFUL

NORMAN.

> PLANTS MAKE WONDERFUL – PETS.

> (**MICHAEL** *and* **JASON** *interrupt* **NORMAN**.)

MICHAEL. Dude, we're gonna get in trouble!

JASON. That squirrel will be fine – he doesn't need all four legs.

MOM. *(offstage)* Michael! Do you know what happened to your good socks, I can't find them and I still have to make three conference calls and one-hundred-forty-four cupcakes.

> (**MOM** *enters with clean clothes and pajamas for the boys.*)

Oh, hello, Jason. Please leave.

JASON. Fine. Bye, Michael. Bye, Michael's Mom.

> (**JASON** *exits.*)

MOM. 'K, bye, don't come back!

MICHAEL. *(chastising her)* Mom!

MOM. Sorry! I mean: Come back anytime, little darling! Milk and cookies and puppy dog tails! Better?

MICHAEL. Much.

MOM. Michael, we have a serious problem, buster. One weeks' worth of your socks have gone missing!

MICHAEL. Nu-uh!

MOM. Uh-huh!

MICHAEL. No way, I know for sure I left them on my night-stand last night.

NORMAN. Then where did they go, Mr. Messy?

MOM. You better find them – otherwise, no broccoli for a week.

MICHAEL. *(thrilled)* Really?!

MOM. By broccoli, I mean video games.

MICHAEL. *(like "Darn It All To Heck")* Gah!

MOM. Oh, don't "Gah" me – and get ready for bed the two of you!

*(**MOM** runs out.)*

MICHAEL. But, I know I left my socks on the nightstand. I'm sure I did! Someone must have taken them. *(spookishly)* Or some thing.

(ominous chord)

NORMAN. You're just trying to scare me.

MICHAEL. I'm serious, Norman. Don't you remember – you said yourself that the stink from my socks was giving you a headache!

(ominous chord)

NORMAN. I did!

MICHAEL. So that means they were there last night. And then they disappeared.

*(**MICHAEL** and **NORMAN** share a series of looks and grunts.)*

NORMAN. Mom didn't take them?

*(**MICHAEL** shakes his head "no" – another ominous chord.)*

NORMAN. Who did?! This sounds like a job for…

*(**NORMAN** pulls something out from underneath his bed – it's a Gorilla Mask, which he puts on!)*

Detective Gorilla!

MICHAEL. Dude, take that monkey mask off – this is serious.

NORMAN. No way! Disguises help me detect better. Now you need your disguise.

MICHAEL. I am not wearing the robot head.

NORMAN. Come on! We always used to do this!

MICHAEL. Yeah, like a whole year ago when I was little.

NORMAN. Please.

MICHAEL. No way.

NORMAN. If you do it, I'll…

> (**NORMAN** *whispers something into* **MICHAEL***'s ear.*)

MICHAEL. Really. Very tempting. How many pickles?

> (**NORMAN** *whispers into* **MICHAEL***'s ear again.*)

For reals?

> (**NORMAN** *nods.*)

Gimme.

> (**NORMAN** *rummages through* **MICHAEL***'s junk pile and pulls out a robot helmet.* **MICHAEL** *puts it on.*)

NORMAN.
ROBOT AND GORILLA AND THE CASE OF THE MISSING
    SOCKS

MICHAEL. Mmmmmmmm. This smells just like me.

NORMAN.
ROBOT AND GORILLA AND THE CASE OF THE MISSING SOCKS

MICHAEL & NORMAN.
ROBOT AND GORILLA AND THE CASE OF THE MISSING SOCKS
ROBOT AND GORILLA AND THE CASE OF THE MISSING SOCKS

NORMAN.
WHERE WOULD I BE IF I WAS A SOCK
WHERE WOULD I TRY TO HIDE?
IN THE CLOSET, IN MY KNAPSACK,
IN A POTTED PLANT OUTSIDE?

WHAT KIND OF CREEP WOULD STEAL A KID'S SOCKS
WHAT A MONSTER HE MUST BE

MICHAEL.
WHEN WE CATCH HIM,
HE'LL REGRET THE DAY HE EVER STOLE FROM ME

NORMAN. Right!

MICHAEL & NORMAN.
ROBOT AND GORILLA AND THE CASE OF THE MISSING SOCKS
ROBOT AND GORILLA AND THE CASE OF THE MISSING SOCKS
ROBOT AND GORILLA AND THE CASE OF THE MISSING SOCKS
ROBOT AND GORILLA AND THE CASE OF THE MISSING SOCKS

MICHAEL.
HERE'S HOW WE WILL SOLVE THE CRIME

NORMAN.
HOW WE GONNA SOLVE IT, CUZ
GORILLA WANNA KNOW

MICHAEL.
PAY ATTENTION CUZ WE HAVEN'T GOT A LOT OF TIME

MICHAEL.
SURE THING, ROBOT
SURE THING, ROBOT

MICHAEL.
FIRST WE NEED ONE OF MY DIRTY SOCKS

(**NORMAN** *hands him a pair.*)

THEN A BALL OF STRING AND SOME SCISSORS, TOO

(**NORMAN** *hands him string and scissors.* **MICHAEL** *cuts a piece of string.*)

TIE ONE END OF THE STRING TO MY DIRTY SOCK

(**MICHAEL** *does so.*)

AND THE OTHER END TO YOU

(**MICHAEL** *ties the string to* **NORMAN** *'s hand.*)

THEN WE GO TO SLEEP
WHEN YOU FEEL THE STRING GO TUG
THEN YOU'LL KNOW WE'VE CAUGHT THE THUG WHO HAS
    BEEN
STEALING ALL MY SOCKS

THEN WE LOCK HIM IN JAIL
AND THROW AWAY THE KEY
AND MY SOCKS WILL AGAIN LIVE PEACFULLY
ALL BECAUSE OF

MICHAEL/NORMAN.

> ROBOT AND GORILLA AND THE CASE OF THE MISSING SOCKS
> ROBOT AND GORILLA AND THE CASE OF THE MISSING SOCKS

MICHAEL.

> COME ON, GORILLA, NOW, LET'S REVIEW
> THE STRING IS TIED TO THE SOCK WHICH IS TIED TO YOU

NORMAN.

> R-O-B-O-T, I THINK I SEE
> THE STRING IS TIED TO THE SOCK WHICH IS TIED TO ME
> AND IF THE STRING IS PULLED OR MOVES AROUND

MICHAEL.

> THEN THE NEFARIOUS SOCK THIEF HAS BEEN FOUND

NORMAN.

> AND IF THE STRING IS MOVED AROUND
> THEN THE MEAN OL' SOCK THIEF HAS BEEN FOUND
> ON ACCOUNT OF

MICHAEL & NORMAN.

> ROBOT AND GORILLA AND THE CASE OF THE MISSING SOCKS
> ROBOT AND GORILLA AND THE CASE OF THE MISSING SOCKS
> ROBOT AND GORILLA … Woo-Hoo!
> ROBOT AND GORILLA … Woo-Hoo!

MICHAEL.

> IT'S TIME TO PUT OUR PLAN IN MOTION

NORMAN.

> NOTHING LEFT TO BE SAID

MICHAEL & NORMAN.

> IT'S TIME TO SOLVE A CASE
> IT'S TIME FOR BED

> (**MICHAEL** *and* **NORMAN** *make their way to their respective beds. The boys throw their heads on the pillow and* **NORMAN** *shuts the light off. Silence.*)

NORMAN. Are you asleep already Michael?

MICHAEL. No.

NORMAN. Can I ask you a question?

MICHAEL. Ok.

NORMAN. Remember that time you used that big word before?

MICHAEL. Which word?

NORMAN. Horty-Cultavist?

MICHAEL. Horticulturist.

NORMAN. Yeah, that one. I have no idea what that means.

MICHAEL. You should know what it means from context clues.

NORMAN. I want *you* to tell me.

MICHAEL. It means someone who is into plants.

NORMAN. Oh, right. Sure. Cool beans. Ha-ha. Michael?

MICHAEL. Yeah.

NORMAN. Is it fun being smart and newly popular?

MICHAEL. It is.

NORMAN. It *is*, great. I had a feeling it was. Michael?

NORMAN. Shut up.

*(Silence. More silence. Then the sound of rustling. The rustling gets more pronounced. Then we hear the sound of a huge slurp. **NORMAN** screams.)*

NORMAN. Michael, Michael, Michael!

MICHAEL. Whoa, whoa, what?!

NORMAN.

WHOA – I SAW IT SUCK UP A SOCK
WHOA – I SAW IT SUCK UP A SOCK
YEAH, I KNOW THAT IT WAS DARK
BUT IT SOUNDED LIKE A SHARK
WITH IT'S CHOMPING AND IT'S CLOMPING AND
I SAW IT, I SAW IT,
I SAW IT, SAW IT SUCK UP A SOCK

MICHAEL. Who?

NORMAN. Your plant!

*(**NORMAN** hits the lights. We see that the sock is gone and the string is sticking out of one of its pods. **MICHAEL** and **NORMAN** both scream. **MOM** and **DAD** come running in.)*

MOM. What's wrong?! What's wrong?!! Use your words!

MICHAEL & NORMAN.
> WE SAW IT SUCK UP A SOCK
> WHOA – WE SAW IT SUCK UP A SOCK
> YEAH, WE KNOW THAT IT SOUNDS NUTS
> BUT YOU BOTH CAN BET YOUR BUTTS
> WE'RE NOT LYING, MOM, I PROMISE, DAD.
> WE SAW IT, SAW IT SUCK UP A SOCK

DAD. Plants can't eat socks, boys. Everyone knows that.

NORMAN. But they can! It was Michael's plant!

MOM. *(joking, of course)* What about your plant? Was he too full from eating your gym shorts?

MICHAEL. Gross, Mom!

NORMAN. Look, I'll show you.

> (**NORMAN** *takes a pair of clean socks and puts one in the center of the floor in between both plants. Silence and stillness and tension.*)

NORMAN. Be very still.

DAD. This is so silly.

MOM. And a huge waste of my valuable time.

NORMAN/MICHAEL. Shhh!

> (*More stillness. Then, suddenly,* **NORMAN**'s *plant comes to life and grabs a sock. Everyone freaks.*)

ALL.
> AHHH! – WE SAW IT SUCK UP A SOCK
> WHOA – WE SAW IT SUCK UP A SOCK
> NEVER KNEW A PLANT COULD EAT
> THINGS THAT YOU WEAR ON YOUR FEET
> THIS IS CRAZY, IT'S AMAZING, GAH!
> WE SAW IT, OH, WE SAW IT, AH
> WE SAW IT, SAW IT SUCK UP A SOCK

MICHAEL. See, we told you!

MOM. *(shocked; at a loss for words)* I think I've forgotten how to speak.

DAD. Honey Get A Hold Of Yourself!

NORMAN. But how come his plant didn't eat the sock?

DAD. What was different about the sock he ate before?

MICHAEL. I've got it! The sock my plant ate before was dirty. The sock Norman's plant just ate was clean!

NORMAN. So your plant only likes gross, stinky socks and my plant only likes clean, sensible socks! I respect that!

MOM. *(putting a halt to things)* No-no-no-no-no-no-no! These things are Not allowed to stay.

NORMAN. But Mom, please!

MOM. No – we have enough picky eaters living here already.

DAD. I mean, where do the socks go after they eat them? That's what I want to know.

MOM. Absolutely not!

MICHAEL. But, Mom, the plants…

MOM. No buts and no plants!

(**MOM** *starts to go.*)

MICHAEL. *(catching* **MOM***)* Well, how about a bargain.

MOM. *(enticed)* A bargain? What kind of bargain?

MICHAEL. If you let us keep the plants…I will *(huge hesitation)* clean my room.

MOM, DAD, & NORMAN. *What?!*

MICHAEL. Oh, don't make me say it again!

MOM. You'll actually clean your room?

NORMAN. And I will personally make sure he keeps his word.

(**MOM** *and* **DAD** *look at each other. A moment.* **DAD** *initiates a huddle. The boys anxiously await.*)

DAD. Well, this doesn't sound like a bad idea.

MOM. No, it's just too risky.

DAD. These plants must sure mean a lot to Michael if he's offering to clean his room. Let's let our boys have this. Just for a little while.

MOM. This whole Michael-cleaning-his-room-thing will save me a lot of time. Alright.

DAD. I love you, dear.

MOM. I know ya do.

> (**MOM** *and* **DAD** *break huddle.*)

DAD. Boys, your mother I have made a decision.

MOM. And that decision is…

MOM & DAD. The plants may stay.

NORMAN & MICHAEL. Yeah!

MOM. Just make sure that no one finds out about these things.

NORMAN. Sure thing, no one'll find out!

MOM. And you'll start cleaning this pig sty immediately?

MICHAEL. *(begrudgingly)* I guess so.

MOM. Michael?

MICHAEL. I mean, Yup-yup-yup! Can't wait!

MOM. Then the horribly scary plants can stay!

> (**MOM** *and* **DAD** *start to leave.*)

DAD. Well, we sure made the right decision, don't you agree?

MOM. You know, I don't know. To be honest – I'm genuinely scared for our lives.

> (**MOM** *and* **DAD** *look at each other. They do not hug. They exit. The boys look at their plants.*)

MICHAEL & NORMAN.
NOW THAT YOU EXIST
I'LL BE THE GREATEST HORTICULTURIST

MICHAEL.
IN MY MY MY MY MY MY MY MY

NORMAN.
MY MY MY MY MY MY MY MY

MICHAEL & NORMAN.
MY MY MY MY MY MY MY MY
ROOM!

Scene Four
Montage

(We are in front of the house, a few days later. **THE NEIGHBORHOOD KIDS** *try to get a glimpse inside.)*

PATTY JENKINS.
I'M NOT NOSY
I'M NO SNOOP
BUT THERE'S SOMETHING GOING ON IN THAT HOUSE

JASON.
THE LAWNS NOT CUT AND THE FLOWERS' DROOP
MONDAY'S PAPER'S STILL SITTING ON THE STOOP

PATTY & JASON.
THERE'S AN EMINATING SMELL THAT SMELLS LIKE
    VEGETABLE SOUP
COMING OUTTA THAT HOUSE

PATTY.
SOMETHING'S GOING ON IN THAT HOUSE

PATTY & JASON.
AND THERE'S A GREEN KINDA WEIRD KINDA GLOW
THAT I SEEN WHEN I PEERED IN THE WINDOW
SOMETHING STRANGE IS GOING DOWN
IT'S THE TALK-A TALK-A TALK OF THE TOWN
IT'S THE TALK-A TALK-A TALK OF THE TOWN

(We are in the bedroom with the boys. **THE PLANTS** *are noticeably bigger.)*

NORMAN. Excuuuuuuuse me. Excuuuuse me. Ex. Ex.

MICHAEL. What are you doing?

NORMAN. I'm teaching Fluffy how to speak.

MICHAEL. *(earnestly)* Oh, cool. *(thinks about it)* Nah! Plants can't speak.

*(***MICHAEL** *feeds his plant a sock.)*

MICHAEL. I can't believe how big they've gotten. Socks must have lots of calories.

*(***NORMAN**'s **PLANT** *shimmies little bit.)*

NORMAN. Alright, alright!

> (**NORMAN** *gets up and takes a fresh sock out the drawer.* **THE PLANT** *rustles with excitement.*)

> But I've got to teach you some manners. You've got to say, "Excuse me, Norman. I'd care for some food now." Try it. Excuuuuuuuse me. Excuuuuuse me.

> (**MICHAEL** *looks at* **NORMAN** *in disbelief.* **NORMAN** *won't give up.*)

MICHAEL. Gimme that!

> (*Finally,* **MICHAEL** *takes the sock out of* **NORMAN**'s *hand and dangles it over the* **PLANT**.)

> Open up!

> (**MICHAEL** *tosses the sock into the* **PLANT**'s *trap.*)

PATTY JENKINS/JASON.
> AND THERE'S A GREEN KINDA WEIRD KINDA GLOW
> THAT I SEEN WHEN I PEERED IN THE WINDOW

JASON/PATTY/NEIGHBOR MAN #1.
> SOMETHING STRANGE GOING DOWN
> IT'S THE TALK-A TALK-A TALK OF THE

> (**THE PLANT** *burps.*)

NORMAN.
> THAT'S THE SIXTEENTH SOCK YOU'VE EATEN TODAY
> I CAN'T KEEP UP ANYMORE
> WE'VE RUN OUT OF FOOD FOR OUR FOOT WARE BUFFET

MICHAEL & NORMAN. (*calling out*)
> MOM WE NEED YOU TO GO TO THE STORE

JASON.
> THE MOM'S BEEN ACTING ESPECIALLY CRACKED
> SOMETIMES SHE COMES HOME WITH AN SUV ENTIRELY
>   PACKED WITH

JASON/PATTY/MOM(OFFSTAGE)/NEIGHBOR MAN #2.
> SOCKS, YES, ONLY SOCKS, I SWEAR THIS WOMAN IS
>   WHACKED
> AND THERE'S SOMETHING GOING ON WITH THAT MOM

(We are in Stop and Save. **MOM** *is at the checkout buying what looks like hundreds of socks. She looks embarrassed and fidgety.)*

MOM.
YOU PROBABLY THINK I'M A NUTBALL
BUYING THIS MANY SOCKS
YOU PROBABLY THINK I'M THE OLD LADY WHO LIVES IN
    THE SHOE
YOU KNOW THE ONE WHO HAD A MILLION CHILDREN, AND
    A COUPLE HUNGRY HOUSE PLANTS TOO
YOU KNOW THE ONE WHO HAD SO MANY FEET TO CLOTHE
SHE DIDN'T KNOW WHAT TO DO
OH, WAIT, I GOTTA COUPON FOR YOU
K, GREAT, BYE BYE TOODLE-LOO

(MOM *runs out of the store.)*

JASON/PATTY/NEIGHBOR MAN #3.
AND THERE'S GREEN KINDA WEIRD KINDA GLOW
THAT I SEEN WHEN I PEERED IN THE WINDOW

(We are back in the room. The **PLANTS** *are even bigger.* **MICHAEL** *is alone in the room, talking to his* **PLANT***. He's sort of stroking it.)*

MICHAEL. You are so cool looking, bud. Your leaves are all…pretty and stuff. Sometimes I wish that I could be nicer looking. Like, I'm a total stud, don't get me wrong, but I'm kind of big and brawny. It might be nice to be soft and delicate, even. You're delicate. Thanks for listening to me talk. I feel like I can just tell you anything, ya know? Like, I can just be who I am. Man, its so good to get these feelings off my chest. *(almost giddy)* I like the way your leaves feel – all tickly!

(NORMAN *storms in and* **MICHAEL** *jumps up, caught.)*

MICHAEL. Whoa-whoa-whoa-HEY. HEY. HEY.

NORMAN. Hey, just needed to get my Solo Man comic book. Sorry. Didn't mean, to, uh, frighten you.

MICHAEL. No, it's fine. *Fine*, really.

(**NORMAN** *is very confused. He leaves.* **MICHAEL** *looks at his* **PLANT**.)

Close one!

JASON/PATTY/NEIGHBOR MAN #4.

TALK-A TALK-A TALK –
TALK-A TALK-A TALK –
TALK-A TALK-A TALK –
TALK-A TALK-A TALK –

SOMETHING STRANGE IS GOING DOWN
SOMETHING STRANGE IS GOING DOWN
SOMETHING STRANGE IS GOING DOWN

(**MOM** *tries to sneak inside the house carrying over-flowing bags of socks.* **PATTY JENKINS** *pops out of the bushes.*)

MOM. Ooh!

PATTY JENKINS. Golly gee, ma'am, that sure is an awful lot of socks!

MOM. Oh, You startled me! It's not that many.

PATTY JENKINS. *(interrupting)* Why so many socks? What is going in that house?

MOM. *("pretending" to be Patty Jenkin's Mom)* Patty Jenkins! – Your mother's calling you, I hear her, and I'm busy and I really must be going.

(**PATTY JENKINS** *gets in front of* **MOM** *and slams the door.*)

PATTY JENKINS. *(suddenly very scary)* When you avoid Patty Jenkins, you annoy Patty Jenkins. And when Patty Gets Annoyed, Patty Gets Nosy.

MOM. Patty, we just have cold feet.

PATTY JENKINS. One year for my birthday, my parents got me a real special gift – but it was a *(making finger quotes)* surprise. I don't like surprises. "What is it?," I asked? "You'll just have to wait and see," they replied. Ignoring me. Avoiding me. Do we remember what happens when you avoid Patty Jenkins?

MOM. You annoy Patty Jenkins.

PATTY JENKINS. *(saying it with her)* …annoy Patty Jenkins, good, good. Later that night, my mother's entire collection of vintage porcelain tea cups was found destroyed. Maybe it was an accident or maybe someone got a little carried away when practicing her new pom-pom routine. Who's to say. Point is: I will stop at nothing until I find out Just What's Going On. I may be pretty as a Pekinese, but I am Bad as a Bulldog.

MOM. Patty, I –

PATTY JENKINS. Call me Bulldog.

MOM. *(getting frantic)* Patty –

PATTY JENKINS. CALL ME BULLDOG!

MOM. *(broken-down and ravaged)* BullDog.

PATTY JENKINS. Good, good. I think you're finally realizing who's in charge here. Look at me.

(**MOM** *does.*)

(both spoken and in sign-language:)

I've got my eyes on you. Grrrrrr.

(a total change of demeanor – she's back to being a bubbly little girl)

Well, I gotta skoot, I think I do hear my mother calling! Bye, Michael's Mom!

(**MOM** *runs inside the house.*)

JASON/NEIGHBOR MAN #4.

SOMETHING STRANGE GOING DOWN
IT'S THE TALK-A TALK-A TALK OF THE TOWN
IT'S THE TALK-A TALK-A TALK OF THE TOWN

*(We are in the bedroom again with the boys. Time has passed. The **PLANTS** are huge now – about four feet tall.)*

NORMAN. Fluffy is already taller than me! After only three weeks!

(**MICHAEL** *goes to his desk.*)

MICHAEL.
> I HATE CLEANING MY
> I HATE CLEANING MY
> I HATE CLEANING MY ROOM

NORMAN. Just keep doing it. Mom's just looking for any excuse to get rid of the boys.

MICHAEL. Well, I'm keeping up my part of the bargain. (**MICHAEL** *goes to his plant and whispers.*) But just know – I'm only doing this for you, buddy. I love you, man.

NORMAN. You do?

MICHAEL. No! I was talkin' to (**MICHAEL** *does "this plant over here" gesture.*)

NORMAN. Oh. Well…No time for love – back to work!

MICHAEL. Grrr –
> I HATE CLEANING MY
> I HATE CLEANING MY
> I HATE CLEANING MY ROOM
> Can't someone just do it for me?

(**MICHAEL**'*s* **PLANT** *lunges across the room.*)

Whoa!

NORMAN. That's no fair! Plant's can't help you!

(**MICHAEL**'*s* **PLANT** *sucks up a dirty sock.*)

MICHAEL. Thanks, dude!

NORMAN. Excuuuuuuuuuuuuse me. Excuuuuuuuuuuuuse me. Fluffy, I think you've got the ability to speak, you're not applying yourself…much like a certain sloppy someone I know.

MICHAEL. I'm applying myself, Norman. I'm trying really hard.

NORMAN. Well…perhaps (*back to* **FLUFFY**)…Ex…Ex…Ex…

MICHAEL. Man. We're almost out of socks again.

NORMAN/**MICHAEL.** Mooooom!

(*We see* **MOM** *at Stop and Save again, looking embarrassed and frazzled, buying socks. We see the neighbors outside the house looking in. We see* **NORMAN** *and* **MICHAEL** *tossing socks into the plants.*)

NORMAN. *(overlapping)*
> EXCUUUUUUUUUSE ME
> EXCUUUUUUUUUSE ME

MOM. *(overlapping)*
> I NEED MORE SOCKS
> WHY CAN'T MY KIDS JUST HAVE A DOG?

PATTY/JASON/DAD. *(overlapping)*
> AND THERE'S GREEN KINDA WEIRD KINDA GLOW
> THAT I SEEN WHEN I PEERED IN THE WINDOW
> AND IT'S NOTHING THAT'S FAMILIAR
> AND IT'S NOTHING THAT WE KNOW

ALL.
> SOMETHING REALLY DIFFERENT
> SOMETHING ALTOGETHER ODD AND OUTLANDISH
> GOING DOWN

PATTY/JASON.
> IT'S THE TALK-A-TALK-A-TALK OF THE
> TALK-A-TALK-A-TALK OF THE

PATTY/JASON/MOM/DAD.
> TALK-A-TALK-A-TALK OF THE

ALL.
> TALK-A-TALK-A-TALK OF THE
> TALK-A-TALK-TALK-TALK-A-TALK-TALK
> TALK-A-TALK-A-TALK-A-TALK-TALK-TALK-TALK

THE PLANTS.
> EX, EX, EX
> EX, EX, EX

> *(Everyone stares at the* **PLANTS***. They just made noise for the first time. Whoa. Total shock.)*

MICHAEL. No way!!!

NORMAN. *(to* **MICHAEL***)* Ha!! I told you!!! *(to* **PLANTS***)* What else have you got to say for yourselves, Boys?

> *(And then, the* **PLANTS** *let out a huge, simultaneous burp.)*

ALL.
> OF THE TOWN!

> *(blackout)*

Scene Five
The Bedroom

(A couple weeks later. the **PLANTS** *are humongous.)*

NORMAN.

CAMPTOWN LADIES SING THIS SONG
DOO-DAH, DOO-DAH
CAMPTOWN LADIES SING THIS SONG

*(***NORMAN*** pauses and points and point to Fluffy to sing
the "Doo-Dah, Doo-Dah, Day," which he does not.)*

MICHAEL. Your plant might be able to speak, but it certainly can't sing.

NORMAN. But Fluffy is the smartest plant I know! He just needs a little practice. Besides, he likes when I sing.

*(***FLUFFY*** rustles his leaves a bit.)*

NORMAN. See?

*(***MOM*** and ***DAD*** enter.)*

DAD. Boys! After four years of being busy at work, your Mother has decided that it's time to take a family vacation.

MICHAEL & NORMAN. Yay!

MOM. All we have to do is pack a bag, alert the mailman, get rid of those life-ruining plants, empty the fridge, –

NORMAN. *(interrupting)* Whoa, whoa. We'd never get rid of the plants.

DAD. Not even for a two week vacation at Skip Badgley's Funtime SuperFun Fun-World Of Tomorrow?

MICHAEL. Skip Badgley's Funtime SuperFun Fun-World Of Tomorrow?! I'd do anything for that!

*(***NORMAN*** glares at ***MICHAEL.***)*

I mean, no. Our place is with the boys.

NORMAN. Yeah!

*(***NORMAN*** crosses the room's center tape live.)*

MICHAEL. Hey, you crossed the line.

(**NORMAN** *peels up the tape.*)

NORMAN. What line?

(*We hear* **JASON** *from offstage.*)

JASON. Where you at, Mikey? Helloooooo?

MICHAEL. Jason's here. Let's talk about this later. Everyone be inconspicuous.

(**JASON** *enters.*)

JASON. Hey fam! Thanks for letting me sleepover tonight.

MOM. Sleepover?! Where? Here? No!

MICHAEL. But Mom, you don't understand, Jason is a notoriously heavy sleeper.

DAD. It does sound like when he sleeps, he sleeps hard.

MOM. True…and Michael and Norman have been so good these last few weeks, I guess they deserve a reward.

NORMAN. Wow. What a great reward.

DAD. Good use of sarcasm, son.

MOM. Now boys – remember. (*She whispers loudly.*) Don't tell him anything about the sock-eating plants. People are starting to get suspicious enough as it is. We don't need this troublemaker blabbing about it.

JASON. What did you call me?

MOM. Nothing, You're hearing things, 'Night Boys!

(**MOM** *and* **DAD** *leave.*)

JASON. Man, your mom is a dingbat sometimes.

NORMAN. Don't call her that, she's our mommy.

JASON. Did you just say, "Mommy?" How old are you, like, two?

MICHAEL. Hey, don't talk to him like that.

(**NORMAN** *looks surprised.* **JASON** *shoots* **MICHAEL** *a look.*)

I mean, Yeah. Norman totally acts like a baby. "Mommy." Ha.

(**JASON** *starts to take his socks off.*)

MICHAEL & NORMAN. No!

JASON. What?!

NORMAN. I… I…thought I saw a ladybug.

JASON. *(making fun of him)* "I thought I saw a ladybug."

> *(He continues taking his socks off.)*

These plants are something else, man. You know, my Uncle Willy is advertising executive assistant apprentice and he'd probably think that these plants are just weird enough to be a lucrative money-making opportunity.

> *(He throws his dirty socks on the ground. We can almost sense **MICHAEL**'s **PLANT** look at the socks longingly.)*

MICHAEL. No, Stanley!

JASON. Who's Stanley?

NORMAN. You named him Stanley?

MICHAEL. Yeah – after Stanley Applejacks, greatest skateboarder of all time. Anyway, you named yours!

NORMAN. Yes, something sensible like Fluffy! Because while my plant may be prickly on the outside, he's warm and fluffy on the inside.

JASON. You guys both have…issues.

> *(**STANLEY** can't contain himself any longer. He lunges for **JASON**'s dirty socks and slurps them up. **JASON** screams.)*

JASON.
I SAW IT SUCK UP A SOCK
WHOA – I SAW IT SUCK UP A SOCK

> *(**MOM** comes in.)*

MOM. What's wrong?!

JASON.
I SAW IT SUCK UP A SOCK
WHOA – I SAW IT SUCK UP A SOCK

MOM. Oh.

NORMAN. Sorry, Mom. That is no way to behave, Stanley.

MICHAEL. He can't help it. He's a growing boy. He needs nutrition.

STANLEY. *(like a puppy whimper)*

EX, EX

JASON. You're talking to your plants! And Your Plants Are Talking Back! I gotta go tell my friends! I gotta go tell the world!

MOM. You are not telling anyone, Jason. What you saw here tonight never happened, got it? And if I ever catch wind that you opened your mouth – I'll feed you to the plants myself.

*(**DAD** enters.)*

DAD. I trust the sleepover is going well.

MOM. Oh, of course it is, Darling, it's fine. Everything's perfect. Just ask young Jason.

JASON. No, you know what, I'm not gonna tell the world about your sock-eating plants.

MICHAEL. Thanks, dude!

JASON. I'm gonna sell my story to The Weird Nation Television Hour and I'm gonna make a million dollars! I'm finally gonna be able to buy my mother a new eye! You people are all freaks and soon everyone is gonna know! Freaks. *FREAKS!*

*(**JASON** runs out. **MOM** looks caught.)*

DAD. Boys, I know this will come as a shock, but, Daddy don't like these plants. They are much too dangerous to have around. They're just too…too…

MOM. They eat socks. They eat socks. Not normal.

*(**MOM** breaks down a bit.)*

DAD. Thank you, honey.

MICHAEL. Don't worry. I can take care of Jason. No one's gonna find out. Even if he did tell The Weird Nation Television Hour, they'd never believe him.

NORMAN. Yeah, Mom – and he's the only one who knows. No one else is gonna find out, right?

(**MOM** *looks off, lost in thought. We see* **PATTY JEN-KINS**.)

PATTY JENKINS. Call me Bulldog. Call me Bulldog.

(**PATTY** *barks several times and disappears.* **MOM** *looks haunted.*)

MOM. As soon as we find a car – yeah, a car – that's big enough to fit them, those plants are going to…the dump.

(*There is a huge flourish of scary organ music.* **MOM** *and* **DAD** *leave.*)

PAPERBOY. (*from offstage*) Incoming!

(*A paper comes flying through the window.*)

NORMAN. What are we gonna do now?

MICHAEL. We need to find a way to keep the boys.

(**NORMAN** *reads the paper.*)

NORMAN. Attention Children and Young Adults of Levitt Lane. This is a reminder that the entry fee for the Levitt Lane All County Science Fair is due at 3pm Monday. Thank you.

(**NORMAN** *puts down the paper.*)

Good to know.

MICHAEL. The science fair!

NORMAN. What does the science fair have to do with anything?

MICHAEL. If we bring the plants to the science fair and win, Mom and Dad will be so proud of us that they'll have to let us keep them.

NORMAN. And we can use the lucrative prize money to buy a spaceship!

MICHAEL. (*like "Great!"*) Impossible!

MICHAEL & NORMAN.

> WHEN WE WIN THE SCIENCE FAIR
> EVERYTHING WILL BE O.K.
> THE PLANTS WILL BE ACCEPTED
> AND THEY'LL BE ALLOWED TO STAY
> AND IF ANYBODY TRIES TO TAKE 'EM WE'LL BE ALL
> NO WAY, JOSE! HEY!

MICHAEL.

> WHEN I WIN THE SCI –

NORMAN.

> WHEN I WIN THE SCI –

BOTH.

> WHEN WE TRIUMPHANTLY WIN THE SCIENCE FAIR
> YEAH!

Scene Six
The Science Fair

(We see **JASON** *on the phone.)*

JASON. Hey, is this the Weird Nation Television Hour with McKenzie Action Phillips Sloan? Well, I've got an incredible story for you. Talking Sock Eating Plants. Yeah, you heard me. Pretty Weeeeeird, right? Well, I'll tell when and where if the price is right. *(a moment)* Yeah, that sounds just fine. The Levitt Lane Science Fair. Tonight. Be there. *(a moment)* My name? Uh… *(Thinks about it. Pause.)* Jason. *(Lightbulb!)* No, uh, I mean, Johnnie SparkleBottoms. My name is Johnnie SparkleBottoms. Yeah, it's Irish. Good luck, McKenzie. Or should I say Happy Plant Hunting. *(hangs up, maniacally)*

(We are outside the science fair.)

PATTY JENKINS.

IT'S THE GREATEST NIGHT OF THE WHOLE STINKIN' YEAR
THE SCIENCE FAIR, THE SCIENCE FAIR
WHY BE ANYWHERE ELSE WHEN YOU COULD BE HERE?
THE SCIENCE FAIR, THE SCIENCE FAIR

(We are inside the Science Fair. A group of science enthusiasts travels from exhibit to exhibit. A **JUDGE** *also wanders around.)*

ALL.

IT'S THE GREATEST NIGHT OF THE WHOLE STINKIN' YEAR
THE SCIENCE FAIR, THE SCIENCE FAIR
WHY BE ANYWHERE ELSE WHEN YOU COULD BE HERE
THE SCIENCE FAIR
THE SCIENCE FAIR!!!

(We see **MICHAEL** *and* **NORMAN**'s *exhibit. They are stationed next to* **PATTY JENKINS** *whose project is covered by a sheet. Above her exhibit reads: "DOMESTICATED BACTERIA: A comparing and contrasting Study of Dirt in the Home." Over the plants is a sign that reads: "REALLY BIG PLANTS." On the other side of*

MICHAEL and NORMAN's exhibit is a huge display on cheese. A diminutive boy named SANJAY stands proudly in front of the exhibit.)

NORMAN. I don't know, some of these projects look really good. Sanjay's Cheese exhibit looks especially impressive.

MICHAEL. But we have enormous, scary plants! That's a million times better than anything else. *(adjusting NORMAN's tie)* Come on dude, this is the science fair. Look sharp!

NORMAN. I'm sorry – I've got more important things to worry about What if people start asking us questions about you know who?

THE PLANTS.

EX, EX

EX, EX

MICHAEL. I know you're hungry – we'll feed you after we win.

NORMAN. That's right, we just have to win and then get the heck outta here!

JUDGE. Now what do we have here, Ms. Jenkins?

PATTY JENKINS. I studied the bacteria levels on items found in the common Suburban home. For your consideration: A tennis racquet. *(She removes a sheet to reveal a tennis racquet.)* A telephone. *(She removes a sheet to reveal a telephone.)* And nastiest of all – a pile of stinky socks! *(She removes a sheet to reveal a pile of socks.)*

(THE PLANTS immediately perk up. They eye PATTY JENKINS's project voraciously.)

NORMAN.

STANLEY'S LOOKING AT PATTY LIKE SHE'S HIS PERSONAL WAITER

MICHAEL.

JUST IGNORE THE SOCKS, DUDE

WE'LL FEED YOU LATER

JUDGE. *(to PATTY JENKINS)* Fascinating, marvelous!

PATTY JENKINS. I know. I'm the best.

(The **JUDGE** *inspects* **PATTY***'s project. We see* **MCKENZIE ACTION PHILLIPS SLOAN** *snake through the crowd.)*

MCKENZIE ACTION PHILLIPS SLOAN. Hello everyone out there in Weeeeeird Nation! This is McKenzie Action Phillips Sloan on the hunt for some completely out of the ordinary Sock-Eating, talking plants!

MICHAEL. We just have to make sure that we don't bring any extra attention to the dudes.

MCKENZIE ACTION PHILLIPS SLOAN. Soon everyone on Levitt Lane will know about these plants!

NORMAN. Well, I think we're doing a pretty OK job at being inconspicuous so far.

MCKENZIE ACTION PHILLIPS SLOAN. And then, Everyone In The World!

MICHAEL. Inconspicuous?

NORMAN. *(goofishly giddy)* I know, right?

JUDGE. Hello, boys. And what have we here?

(As **NORMAN** *talks to the* **JUDGE***,* **FLUFFY** *and* **STANLEY** *attempt to lunge for* **PATTY JENKINS***'s socks.* **MICHAEL** *jumps back and forth between both* **PLANTS** *trying to make sure they don't lunge.)*

NORMAN. Well, these are our pet plants.

JUDGE. Pet. Plants. You perplex me. As does your project. Although, it certainly seems to be attracting lots of attention. Perhaps it's because it's the tallest exhibit.

NORMAN. No Giraffe Exhibit this year, huh?!

JUDGE. I don't find you at all funny.

(As **MICHAEL** *is trying to hold back* **FLUFFY***,* **STANLEY** *makes a quick move and snatches one of* **PATTY JENKINS***'s socks. No one notices, but the* **JUDGE** *flips around, having heard something.)*

NORMAN. [ad lib to cover]

MICHAEL. No, no, no, no, no!

JUDGE. What did you say?

MICHAEL. Nothing!

JUDGE. I heard something.

MICHAEL. I think it was the wind, sir.

JUDGE. Suspicious little people.

(*The* JUDGE *walks over to the next exhibit.*)

NORMAN. What happened?!

MICHAEL. He ate a sock off of Patty's project!

NORMAN. Maybe Patty won't notice.

(PATTY *lets out a blood-curdling scream.*)

PATTY JENKINS. One of my socks is missing!

JUDGE. What's this?

PATTY JENKINS. Someone stole one of the socks off of my exhibit – Vandals! Vandals!

JUDGE. Oh, spare me the theatrics, Patty Jenkins. It's got to be around here somewhere.

(JUDGE *and* PATTY JENKINS *inspect the area around the project.*)

NORMAN. What do we do now?

MICHAEL. I've got an idea!

(MICHAEL *takes off his shoe and removes a sock off his foot.* NORMAN *gags and the plants sort of wilt for a moment – the smell is intense.* MICHAEL *throws the nasty sock on* PATTY JENKINS*'s exhibit.* JUDGE *and* PATTY *look up.*)

JUDGE. Why there it is, Patty Jenkins. Looks like you need to get your eyes checked, because you're blind.

(JUDGE *wanders back over to another near-by exhibit.*)

PATTY JENKINS. But that wasn't there before. I know it wasn't. You two had something to do with this!

NORMAN. No!

PATTY JENKINS. I know you did and I'm gonna find out! Patty Jenkins Get Angry!

MCKENZIE ACTION PHILLIPS SLOAN. We've received word that the mutant plants are located in the Northwest Corner of the gymnasium! Let's descend!

JUDGE. Oh no. My socks have fallen. You know nothing gets me all bothered like when my socks have fallen. It just drives me crazy, I mean doesn't it drive you crazy?, etc.

(**JUDGE** *puts his leg up on Sanjay's stool. His pant leg hikes up, revealing a gloriously white sock which he pulls up and tugs on to make his point.* **FLUFFY** *shakes with hunger and begins to snake towards the sock.* **MICHAEL** *and* **NORMAN** *don't notice, but* **PATTY JENKINS** *does.*)

PATTY JENKINS. The Plant! The Plant!

(**FLUFFY** *snaps back to his "just your average, humungous plant" position.*)

JUDGE. What are you saying?

PATTY JENKINS. The plant looked like it wanted to…like it wanted to eat your sock!

JUDGE. Insufferable, hysterical girl – insane accusations are frowned upon here at the Levitt Lane All County Science Fair.

PATTY JENKINS. But, I saw it! I saw it!

JUDGE. Impossible!

(**THE PLANTS** *begin to shake. We've never seen them shake like this before.*)

NORMAN. (*to* **MICHAEL**) Dude what's going? I've never seen them shake like this?

MICHAEL. I don't know, I think they're sick!

PATTY JENKINS. I think they're gonna puke!

JUDGE. Tell me this – what do you feed these plants to get them to be so big?

NORMAN. Well…

JUDGE. Yes?

MICHAEL. Well…

JUDGE. Yes?

MICHAEL/NORMAN. Well…

JUDGE. Yes?

> *(Together, the* **PLANTS** *let out a simultaneous burp and out of their traps comes flying some previously-eaten socks.)*

JUDGE. *SOCKS!*

> *(The* **PLANTS** *regain composure and then, BAM, eat the socks they just coughed onto the table. Everyone screams.* **MCKENZIE ACTION PHILLIPS SLOAN** *runs over with his crew.)*

MCKENZIE ACTION PHILLIPS SLOAN. Here they are! Weird! Weird!

> *(Over the following, a huge commotion erupts. People gather and the plants begin to freak, jutting every which way in fits of nervous plant-spasms. They knock over* **PATTY JENKINS**'s *project.* **PATTY JENKINS** *screams, the boys try to hold the plants back.* **MCKENZIE** *snaps pictures. There is general pandemonium.)*

PATTY JENKINS. *(overlapping)* I told you! I told you I saw them!

NORMAN. It was an accident!

MCKENZIE ACTION PHILLIPS SLOAN. This is McKenzie Action Phillips Sloan reporting live from the Levitt Lane All County Science Fair where two unimportant boys just unveiled their new, horrible, totally weird plants!

MICHAEL. We unveiled nothing! *(to the camera)* We unveiled nothing!

NORMAN. These plants aren't supposed to be put on display – they are our pets!

JUDGE. Plants as pets?! That's preposterous! Quiet! Quiet! Quiet!

> *(The* **JUDGE** *quiets down the pandemonium and the hubbub.)*

You have made a mockery of the Science Fair!

MICHAEL. Leave him alone! These plants are *our* pets – and we stand by them! No matter what anybody thinks.

NORMAN. Really?

MICHAEL. Really.

PATTY JENKINS. You're both losers, then! Weird losers!

MICHAEL. Well you smell like eggs!

NORMAN. Finally, someone's said it!

JUDGE. Fine. I will reward your loyalty and gumption with a heaping cup of *Disqualification.*

SANJAY. Which is defined by the Levitt Lane Heritage Dictionary as No Longer Being Allowed To Participate in the Science Fair!

*(**SANJAY** gives a proud humph.)*

JUDGE. Thank you, Sanjay.

NORMAN. But we needed to win!

MICHAEL. So that Fluffy and Stanley can stay with us!

JUDGE. You are hereby banished from the gymnasium –

MICHAEL & NORMAN. No!

JUDGE. From the Science Fair!

MICHAEL & NORMAN. No!

JUDGE. And from the school!

NORMAN. You mean –

JUDGE. That's right. EXPELLED.

*(There is a crash of thunder. Everyone laughs and sneers at the boys. **JUDGE** runs out.)*

MCKENZIE ACTION PHILLIPS SLOAN. Judge! Judge! How about giving an exclusive interview to The Weird Nation Television Hour?!

*(**MCKENZIE** runs out.)*

PATTY JENKINS. Wait! Interview me! I'm the great big deal!

*(**PATTY** runs out, leaving the boys alone. **NORMAN** looks beaten.)*

NORMAN. Aye-yay-yay. (**NORMAN** *begins to panic.*) What's gonna happen now? What are we gonna do?

MICHAEL. Dude, it's OK.

NORMAN. *(in a fit of panic)* Oh, Aye-yay-yay, aye-yay-yay, aye-yay-yay!

MICHAEL. *Norman.* Chill, please.

(**NORMAN** *does.*)

Can I say something to you?

NORMAN. Will it make me aye-yay-yay?

MICHAEL. I don't think so.

NORMAN. Ok then.

(At some point during the following, **MOM** *enters, unseen by* **MICHAEL** *and* **NORMAN**, *and watch their sons be cool with each other.)*

MICHAEL.

I USED TO THINK YOU WERE A LITTLE WIMP
AN ANNOYING, TINY ELF
GEEKY TO THE EXTREME, WITH A WOMANLY SCREAM,
ALWAYS DOIN' STUFF ALL BY YOURSELF

BUT THESE LAST FEW WEEKS THAT WE'VE SPENT
   TOGETHER
HAVE BEEN LOTS OF FUN FOR ME
THEY'VE TOTALLY MADE ME SEE
YOU'RE PRETTY FUNNY
YOU'RE ALMOST COOL
YOU'RE HALFWAY NOT-AT-ALL-A-LOSER
YOU VAUGLEY RULE

AND YOU'RE A GOOD, GOOD BROTHER
YEAH, I GUESS YOU'RE SORTA KINDA NOT SO BAD

NORMAN.

I USED TO THINK YOU WERE A BIG FAT CHIMP
CAUSE YOU NEVER SEEMED TO REALLY CARE
EVERY TIME WE GOT CLOSE, I'D THINK, WOOF!
HE SMELLS GROSS
BUT NOW I'M GLAD THE SMELL IS THERE

MICHAEL.

THE SMELL WILL ALWAYS BE RIGHT THERE, BROTHER,

    BROTHER

MICHAEL & NORMAN.
    YOU'RE PRETTY FUNNY
    YOU'RE ALMOST COOL
    YOU'RE HALFWAY NOT-AT-ALL-A-LOSER
    YOU VAGUELY RULE

    AND YOU'RE A GOOD, GOOD BROTHER
    YEAH, I GUESS YOU'RE SORTA KINDA NOT SO BAD

    YOU'RE FAIRLY PLEASANT
    YOU'RE ALMOST FINE
    YOU'RE MAYBE TOLERABLE
    I'M GLAD YOUR MINE
    AND YOU'RE A GOOD, GOOD BROTHER
    YEAH, I GUESS YOU'RE SORTA KINDA NOT SO BAD

    YEAH, YOU'RE A GOOD, GOOD BROTHER
    UNLIKE ANY OTHER
    YOU'RE A GOOD, GOOD BROTHER BECAUSE

    YOU'RE SORTA KINDA TOTALLY THE BEST BROTHER THAT
        THERE EVER WAS

MOM. Oh, boys!

NORMAN. Mom, what are you doing here?

MOM. Your father and I saw you on the TV!

    (**MICHAEL** *makes an "Ugh" sound.*)

MOM. Boys, I'm so proud of you.

NORMAN. Thanks Mom!

MOM. I love you boys for exactly who you are. Even if you
    do have weirdo pets.

MICHAEL. You'll love us no matter what?

MOM. Sure will!

NORMAN. Even if we're…

    (**JUDGE** *bursts in.*)

JUDGE. *Expelled!…*

    (*Everyone gasps.*)

    …is exactly what you're not going to be!

(Everyone cheers.)

JUDGE. *(cont.)* Why, as I sat in my solitary chamber, cold and alone, I thought to myself: I wish I had a brother. I wish I had someone who cared enough to stick up and fight for me. And then my ugly old eyes sunk and caught a glimpse of my desk plant. I found comfort in the green gaze of that hibiscus, and, well, it made me feel better! *(announcing it to everyone)* It Made Me Feel Better!

(Everyone cheers.)

Oh, sweet sweet boys, not only are you back in the science fair, but as the official judge of the Levitt Lane All County Science Fair, I hereby award your project… Second Place!

PATTY JENKINS. Clearly, I won.

JUDGE. Ah, Patty Jenkins, Yes, Yes, Yes… *No you did not.*

PATTY JENKINS. What didn't I do?

JUDGE. Patty Jenkins, this time you did NOT win.

PATTY. *(with a smile.)* Oh. I'm gonna get crazy and break things now.

> **(PATTY** *runs out. We hear a crash offstage.* **PATTY** *returns with a smile.)*

NORMAN. Who did win?

JUDGE. Benny Dyke. He built a baking soda volcano. *Nothing* beats a baking soda volcano.

MICHAEL. Well, that's quite all right, sir!

MOM. I can't believe you didn't win. Let's go steal the first place trophy.

NORMAN. No, Mom. We're more than happy with second place!

PLANTS.
> EX, EX
> EX, EX

MOM. I wish your father was here to see this!

DAD. I've been parking the car!

MICHAEL/NORMAN. Dad / Daddy!

DAD. Boys!

MOM. Honey, wonderful things have happened.

DAD. I heard in the parking lot. Oh, how I love my boys who love plants who are weird and different.

MOM. Great!

DAD. And that's not all – look who I found skulking in the bushes outside.

(*JASON enters.*)

JASON. Hey friends!

DAD. Boys, Jason's transformed.

JASON. *(to MICHAEL)* I'm sorry I sold your story to The Weird Nation Television Hour. *(to NORMAN)* And I'm sorry I made fun of you and called you freakzoid and dweebface and so on and so forth.

MICHAEL. Apology accepted, man. Norman?

(**NORMAN** *thinks on it.*)

NORMAN. Put 'er there, pal.

MICHAEL. So, why the sudden total change of heart?

JASON. Because everybody loves you guys now! Being nerdy and weird and full of heart is the new cool!

NORMAN. That's not really a good reason to change, but I suppose it's a step in the right direction!

MOM. I don't think Jason's the only one who has got some apologizing to do.

(*Everyone looks at* **PATTY JENKINS.**)

PATTY JENKINS. Me?

(**PATTY JENKINS** *runs out.*)

DAD. She's just so horrible.

NORMAN. So, Mom and Dad. There's still the question of The Boys.

MICHAEL. Can they live with us forever and ever?

MOM. Well…

DAD. Uh…

MOM. Boys, we don't know how to tell you this, but…

DAD. Stanley…

MOM. …and Fluffy…

MOM & DAD. Can stay!

> *(Everyone cheers.)*

MOM. And not only that, but we have a special surprise!

MICHAEL. What Kind of surprise?

MOM. Oh, nothing too big. Just a two week family vacation to Skip Badgley's Funtime SuperFun Fun-World Of Tomorrow!

EVERYONE. *(joining her)* Skip Badgley's Funtime SuperFun Fun-World Of Tomorrow! Yeah!!

MICHAEL. But how on Earth are we gonna get the boys there?

MOM. We're buying a Gargantuan Brown Winnebago! Just for the plants!

ALL. Yeah!!!

DAD. But how will we be able to afford that?

MOM. We're selling your golf clubs!

DAD. Great!

ALL. Yeah!!!

JASON.

> I GUESS, PLANTS MAKE BACK-YOU-UP-FULLY AND
> NEVER-WILL-BULLY-YOU FRIENDS

DAD.

> IT'S THE LATEST OF TRENDS

MICHAEL & NORMAN.

> PLANTS MAKE WONDERFUL

MOM.

> SOME PEOPLE CAN'T HAVE A BIRD
> CUZ BIRD'S MAKE 'EM SNIFFLE AND SNEEZE

DAD.

> OTHERS THINK FISH ARE BEST SERVED ON A DISH

MOM/DAD.

    AND OTHERS HATE DOGS ON ACCOUNT OF THE FLEAS

PATTY JENKINS.

    FINE!

    PLANTS MAKE PERFECTLY PRICKLY

    PLEASANTLY TICKLY PETS

MICHAEL & NORMAN.

    EVERYBODY FORGETS

    PLANTS MAKE WONDERFUL PETS

ALL.

    PLANTS MAKE FREAKISHLY MAZE-Y,

    AND VINY AND CRAZY GOOD PETS

    EVERYBODY FORGETS

    A PLANT NEVER BARKS OR UPSETS

    CUZ PLANTS MAKE WONDERFUL

    PLANTS MAKE WONDERFUL

THE PLANTS.

    DOO-DAH

    DOO-DAH

ALL.

    DOO-DAH

    DOO-DAH

THE PLANTS.

    DOO-DAH

    DOO-DAH

NORMAN/MICHAEL. Ready? Go!

ALL.

    LA LA LA LA LA LA LA LA

    LA LA LA LA LA LA LA

    LA LA LA LA LA LA

    PLANTS MAKE WONDERFUL –

    LA LA LA LA LA LA LA LA

    LA LA LA LA LA LA LA

    LA LA LA LA LA LA

    PLANTS MAKE WONDERFUL –

    LA LA LA LA LA LA LA LA

    LA LA LA LA LA LA LA

LA LA LA LA LA LA

ALL. *(cont.)*

PLANTS MAKE WONDERFUL –
PLANTS MAKE WONDERFUL –
PLANTS MAKE WONDERFUL –

PETS!
YEAH!!!

(blackout)

The End

www.ingramcontent.com/pod-product-compliance
Lightning Source LLC
Chambersburg PA
CBHW050627070726
47592CB00028B/1706